ISBN 978-1-330-99201-2
PIBN 10130800

This book is a reproduction of an important historical work. Forgotten Books uses
state-of-the-art technology to digitally reconstruct the work, preserving the original format
whilst repairing imperfections present in the aged copy. In rare cases, an imperfection in
the original, such as a blemish or missing page, may be replicated in our edition. We do,
however, repair the vast majority of imperfections successfully; any imperfections that
remain are intentionally left to preserve the state of such historical works.

1 MONTH OF
FREE
READING

at

www.ForgottenBooks.com

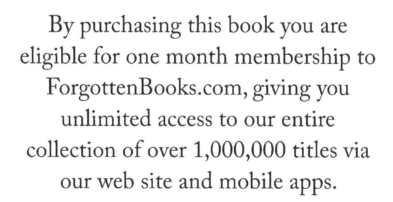

By purchasing this book you are eligible for one month membership to ForgottenBooks.com, giving you unlimited access to our entire collection of over 1,000,000 titles via our web site and mobile apps.

To claim your free month visit:

www.forgottenbooks.com/free130800

English
Français
Deutsche
Italiano
Español
Português

www.forgottenbooks.com

Mythology Photography **Fiction**
Fishing Christianity **Art** Cooking
Essays Buddhism Freemasonry
Medicine **Biology** Music **Ancient**
Egypt Evolution Carpentry Physics
Dance Geology **Mathematics** Fitness
Shakespeare **Folklore** Yoga Marketing
Confidence Immortality Biographies
Poetry **Psychology** Witchcraft
Electronics Chemistry History **Law**
Accounting **Philosophy** Anthropology
Alchemy Drama Quantum Mechanics
Atheism Sexual Health **Ancient History**
Entrepreneurship Languages Sport
Paleontology Needlework Islam
Metaphysics Investment Archaeology
Parenting Statistics Criminology
Motivational

STORY

FOR THE

FOURTH OF JULY

BY UNCLE NED.

AN EPITOME OF AMERICAN HISTO
ADAPTED TO INFANT MINDS.

NEW YORK:

KIGGINS & KELLOGG,

123 & 125 William St.

FOR THE

FOURTH OF JULY,

BY UNCLE NED.

AN EPITOME OF AMERICAN HISTORY,
ADAPTED TO INFANT MINDS.

NEW YORK:
KIGGINS & KELLOGG.
123 & 125 William St.

STORY

FOR

THE FOURTH OF JULY.

THE Fourth of July was a holyday looked forward to by all the children of the village where Uncle Ned resided, with as joyful anticipations almost as Christmas or New-Year's. On "Independence day," the largest liberty was allowed. The boys who were large and wary enough to be safely trusted with them, were permitted to amuse themselves with fire-crackers, torpedoes, and other miniature fireworks; while the little girls were treated with a walk to the bon-bon and toy-shops and juvenile book-stores, with their pockets supplied by the generous-hearted old man with the means of buying whatever their fancy suggested. On that day, too, Harry Bluff, who thought himself the bravest boy in the whole village, would bring out his little cannon, load it with powder, and fire it off with so much spirit that Uncle Ned would often say, "That boy anticipates being a soldier."

After they had become tired with play, Uncle Ned would gather them together, under

the shade of the large old elm that stands before his door, and relate to them some interesting story of the "days that tried men's souls," when he fought and bled for the privileges they were enjoying—or tell them some tale of an earlier period, when he was a child like themselves.

On one Fourth of July, he promised the smaller children to narrate to them the cause of the day being set aside as a universal holyday; and, gathering his young audience about him, and adapting his language to their infant minds (Uncle Ned had a happy faculty for that), he proceeded as follows:—

"Four hundred years ago, my dear children, the people

across the wide Atlantic, three thousand miles from here, did not imagine there was such a beautiful country as this, till Christopher Columbus ventured upon the wide ocean, and after sailing many days, discovered the 'New World.'

Columbus on the Ocean.

At that period, where we now see beautiful farms, there was nothing but woods, inbahited by wild beasts; and in the place of the fine houses and the comforts of civilized life which we enjoy, there was nothing but here and there a wigwam, inhabited by savages, who when they saw Columbus' vessel approach, were so alarmed they fled.   He landed first on one of the West India islands, and soon after other places were discovered along the coasts of North and South America.

"The people from the old countries soon came over, attracted hither, as many now are to California, by the stories they heard of the abundance of gold and silver in this coun-

try. Some of those who settled here were able to stay and form settlements, where their descendants remain to this day. Others, in North America, although they came in large companies, were killed by the Indians, or died by sickness, so that their settlement came to nothing.

"About two hundred years ago, there were people in England called 'puritans.' They were so called because they tried to be *pure*, or to leave off everything they thought not right. But most of the people of England did not love the puritans, and would not allow them to worship and serve God as they wished. So after they had suffered a great deal, they removed over to Holland, and said they would live among the Dutch, if they could be free to serve God. The Dutch let them have their own way about their religion ; but many of the Dutch did not fear God, and the puritans said their children would be corrupted and spoiled if they grew up and lived there. So they concluded to come to this country, and live in the wilderness, where they might serve God, and bring up their children to serve him, and establish an empire, with laws founded on the Bible. They did not come to get money, but to be puritans and good men, and make their children good.

"It was for *you*, children, that they were willing to take

all this trouble; they thought of *you*, and of *all* of us who are now living here, when they agreed to come here over the mighty waters. Well, our fathers set sail to come to this country, and they intended to land where New York is now, and settle on the banks of the Hudson river; for the land is good there. But the Dutch wanted all that country, and they hired the captain of their ship not to carry them there, but to bring them away to the north. The wicked captain detained them a great while, but at last they landed at a place they called Plymouth, on the twenty-second of December, in the year of our Lord one thousand six hundred and twenty.

" There, they were without any house, in the middle of the winter, a great part of their provisions spent, and savage Indians all around them. Their sufferings were so great that forty-eight of them died before spring. How easy it would have been for the Indians to kill them all! But God turned their hearts so that they did not; for God loved the puritans, and he meant they should live here, and serve him in all generations. Some of the Indians wanted to kill them, but God raised them up a friend. Massasoit, a chief, whose name every child should remember, said, ' No, you shall not kill the English till you first kill me ;' and so God preserved them alive. And God was a friend to them and their children ; and he protected them, and others who came over and filled the land.

" The people, of what is now the United States, were under the same government as the people of England. But the king and parliament wanted to tax our people, and make them pay a good deal of money, when they would not let them send over anybody to take part in making the laws. That was unjust and wicked, and our people would not do so. They loved the king of England, and would obey him, if he would do right by them ; but they would not let him oppress them and their children, and deprive them of their rights. Then the king was angry, and sent over armies to fight them, and compel them to submit.

"It was at that time that our fathers sent their wisest and best men to Philadelphia, to meet in congress, and see what the country must do. And at last the congress agreed they would have nothing more to do with the king of England, but they and the whole country would make their own laws, and be *independent*. They declared this openly to the world, on the fourth day of July, one thousand seven hundred and seventy-six. This is what we mean by *Independence;* and this is what makes the fourth of July a great and memorable day. The war continued five or six years longer; but God was on our side, and disappointed all the hopes of the king, so that he at last consented, and the United States have ever since been independent; and I trust, my dear children, they will ever remain so, united and enduring as the ROCK OF AGES."

CPSIA information can be obtained
at www.ICGtesting.com
Printed in the USA
BVHW040821220219
540922BV00024B/2883/P